CLEVER KARLIS

To my father, Scott McCrossen. - J.M.

Printed in the United States of America.   ISBN 0-8167-4024-0
10 9 8 7 6 5 4 3 2 1

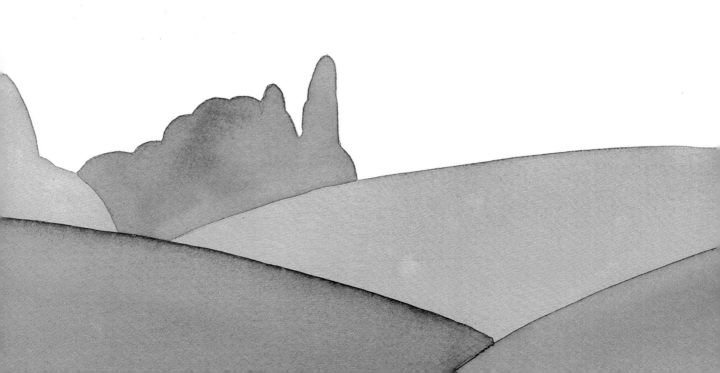

LEGENDS OF THE WORLD

CLEVER KARLIS

A LATVIAN LEGEND

RETOLD BY JAN MIKE   ILLUSTRATED BY CHARLES REASONER

TROLL

Beyond three-times-nine mountains, beyond three-times-nine seas, in the three-times-ninth kingdom, lived a young man named Karlis, who decided it was time to go into the world.

Karlis had scarcely left his humble village when he came upon a tall man resting his long legs under a gnarled old apple tree.

"Good day," the lad said. "Who are you?"

The man opened drowsy eyes and yawned. He stood, and Karlis saw he had huge, heavy millstones strapped to each of his feet.

"I am called Fleetfoot," the man answered. "I wear these stones to slow me down, for I would circle the world like that"— the man snapped his fingers—"if not for their weight."

"I am Karlis, and I am off to seek my fortune," said the lad. "Will you join me?"

Fleetfoot agreed to join forces with Karlis.

Past the old apple tree and into the forest they walked. Near the edge of the forest Karlis spotted a giant uprooting two huge trees, one with each hand.

"I am Strongarm," the giant explained. "I've gathered these switches to make a broom for my cave."

"Would you care to join us?" Karlis asked the giant. "We are off to seek our fortunes."

Strongarm tossed his trees aside and joined them.

Through the forest the group went, until they came to a clearing. In the center of the clearing an archer stood, aiming his bow at the horizon.

"Don't waste your arrows," Karlis said. "We've seen no animals here."

"I am Sharpshooter," the archer replied. "Nine miles from here a deerfly nips at the tail of a small doe. I thought I would help her."

As Sharpshooter let his arrow fly, Fleetfoot tore off his millstones. In less than a breath he was gone, and in a full breath he returned, holding Sharpshooter's arrow.

"The little doe thanks you," Fleetfoot said. He handed the arrow to Karlis, a dead deerfly neatly speared on its tip.

"Surely we are meant to be a team," Karlis said, handing the arrow to Sharpshooter in turn. "Come seek your fortune with us, Sharpshooter."

Sharpshooter agreed, and the four men walked on.

At the edge of the clearing a sudden gust of wind tore at their ragged clothes. Resting against a granite boulder, an old man blew through his half-covered mouth toward a whirling windmill.

"What are you doing?" Karlis asked.

"I am called Windmover. I'm grinding barley for my morning cake," the old man answered.

"Why do you cover your mouth?"

"Too much wind would destroy my mill. Will you eat with me?"

After a breakfast of barley cakes and clear water, Windmover agreed to join the others.

he next morning they arrived in a bustling city and found the streets packed with excited crowds. Karlis and his men followed the crowds to a castle. In the middle of the courtyard stood a large group of richly dressed merchants and nobles.

Karlis asked why all these wealthy men had been gathered together. A plump baker laughed and told him that the royal Princess Evelina's councillors had decreed that she must marry. She had asked all of the eligible men to compete in games of strength and skill. The leader of the winning team would be her husband.

"Is the princess a simpleton?" Karlis asked. "Is that why the council decrees she must marry?"

"No woman can rule on her own," the baker rumbled. "The princess needs a wise man to guide her."

Karlis raised a skeptical eyebrow and turned away.

"Shall we compete?" he asked his men.

"Do you wish to marry the princess?" Windmover asked in return.

"No, but the princess does not wish to marry me, either," said Karlis. "Perhaps we can come to an agreement."

Windmover nodded, then sat and closed his eyes. "Perfect place to rest," he said. "Wake me when all the fuss is over."

Valerijis, head of the ruling council, sneered when Karlis registered his ragged band of men. All around the courtyard, nobles and merchants laughed at the group, until finally Princess Evelina arrived with a fanfare of trumpets.

Karlis carefully studied the princess. He and his men might be able to earn their fortune by helping her. Evelina's cheeks were pink, and she bit at her lower lip as the competitors gathered before her. Her dark hair drifted in the breeze, and in her black eyes Karlis saw a spark of anger.

Valerijis ordered the archers to assemble for the first contest. Soon bowstrings hummed like bees as each archer shot arrows into a line of targets, struggling to hit the farthest one.

Sharpshooter waited until the rest of the archers had no more arrows. Then he pulled one long arrow from his quiver and strung it. Swift and sure, his arrow pierced the center of the first target, then the second, and the third. Finally it slammed into the far wall with the entire row of targets strung along its shaft.

Karlis saw the princess smile as Valerijis grudgingly awarded the prize for archery to Sharpshooter.

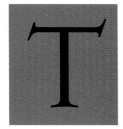he next competition was a contest of strength. Marble blocks were stacked in the middle of the courtyard. Each block was the weight of two grown men. Valerijis rang a bell, and the yard filled with huffing and puffing as strong men from each team tried to lift a single block.

"This is getting dull," Strongarm finally shouted. He strode out and stacked the blocks into a tall tower, then lifted the entire tower easily in his left hand. With his right hand he grasped the other strong men and tossed them to the top of the tower, where they cowered in fear.

"Put them down!" Valerijis shouted.

"Very well!" Strongarm released the marble blocks with such precision that they landed upright, each block holding a trembling man.

Karlis heard the princess laugh out loud as Valerijis unwillingly awarded the strength competition to Strongarm.

Strongarm sat down next to Windmover as the final contest was announced, a footrace nine miles down a winding road to a pond. Each group was given a clay jar. The first to return with a full water jar would win.

"I will run in this race," Princess Evelina said, and she stepped out of her long skirt. A gasp echoed through the crowd as the merchants and nobles saw that the princess was wearing pants.

"But, your highness..." Valerijis stammered.

"Do you expect me to marry a man who cannot beat me in a simple footrace?" The princess took a water jar in one hand.

Karlis smiled. He was beginning to like this princess, and he thought he knew what her plan was.

"Run, Fleetfoot," he whispered.

Fleetfoot grabbed his jar and threw off his millstones. In less than a minute he was out of sight.

Karlis waited. Finally he spoke.

"Sharpshooter, look down the road and tell me what you see."

Sharpshooter raised one hand and peered into the distance.

"Fleetfoot has already filled his jar. But he stopped to rest under an apple tree.... Oh, no!"

"What happened?"

"The princess just ran by and emptied Fleetfoot's jar."

"Wake him!" Karlis said.

Sharpshooter lifted his bow and let an arrow fly. He peered once more, then he laughed.

"What happened?"

"My arrow pierced an apple, which fell on Fleetfoot's head. He has run back to refill his jar."

Sharpshooter had scarcely finished speaking when Fleetfoot returned. In his left hand he carried the full water jar and in his right an arrow-pierced apple.

Princess Evelina was the next runner to return. She frowned when she saw Fleetfoot's full water jar but held her peace as Valerijis reluctantly decreed that Karlis and his team had won the competition.

Karlis ignored the angry mutters of the dispersing nobles and merchants. He watched Princess Evelina as she returned to her castle, shoulders slumped.

Later that evening, while the whole court celebrated, Karlis and the princess sat alone at the head of the table.

"Why are you so quiet?" Karlis asked.

"I do not wish to marry," the princess answered.

"Is that why you poured the water out of Fleetfoot's jar?"

Princess Evelina nodded. "I thought no one could run faster than I. If I had won the race, then the council would have had to free me from their decree."

Karlis looked toward the council seats. Valerijis was watching them with angry eyes. He turned back to the princess.

"Perhaps," he said. "Or perhaps they would have ordered you to marry... someone else."

He leaned forward and whispered.

"I don't wish to marry, either," he told the princess. "I will happily set you free, but we must make sure that the council cannot trap you again."

Evelina smiled up at Karlis, and they began to whisper. By the time the meal was over, Karlis had a plan.

That night he set his men to work sewing a huge sack. The following morning, when the whole court had gathered, Karlis announced to Valerijis that he did not wish to marry the princess. He wanted another reward.

Valerijis smiled. "I will give you all the gold you can carry if you will leave us in peace," he said.

"I graciously accept the decree of the council," Karlis said.

He ordered his men to lay out the huge sack. Valerijis turned purple with anger as Karlis and the others stuffed the bag full of gold and treasure. Then Strongarm tossed the bag over his shoulder.

s Karlis and his men left the castle, Valerijis shouted for the army to assemble. Council members ran to the stables, and soldiers grabbed their weapons. Within an hour, Valerijis and the council led the soldiers after Karlis. Princess Evelina jumped on her horse and followed.

Warned of the approaching army by Sharpshooter, Karlis ordered his men to the top of a tall hill. There he waited, looking out over the green countryside.

When they arrived, Valerijis ordered the soldiers to stay at the base of the hill. He and the council rode to the top, followed by the princess.

"Return the gold that you stole," Valerijis shouted.

"We stole nothing," Karlis said. "We took only what you gave us."

"Give it all back, or I will order my army to destroy you," Valerijis demanded.

Karlis turned to Evelina. "Is this your wish, Princess?"

"No," she answered firmly. "The councillors have broken their word and cannot be trusted. I will gladly be rid of them and rule with a new council."

"Very well." Karlis grabbed Princess Evelina's hand, and he signaled to Windmover.

The old man opened his mouth wide, and before Valerijis and his council could react, a huge wind swept them aloft. As their bright robes filled with air, they bobbed about like giant silk balloons. Then Windmover puffed again, and the entire council was blown away beyond the farthest hills.

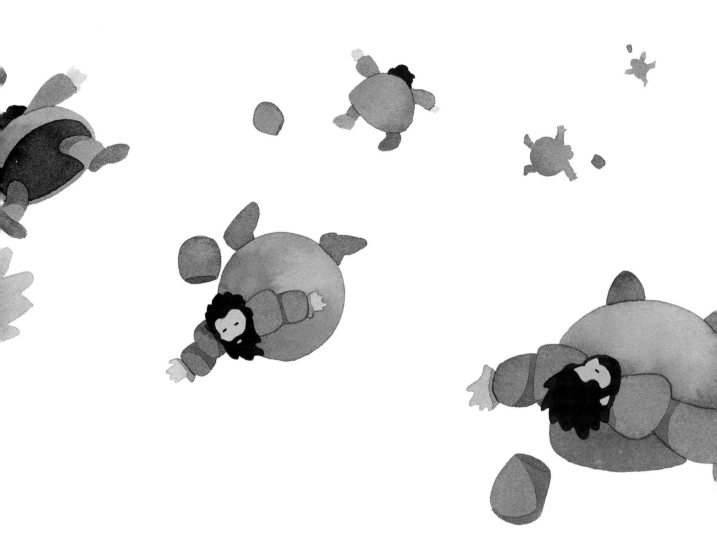

Princess Evelina clapped her hands and smiled, but before she could speak, Karlis kneeled at her feet.

"Please accept the return of your gold, my princess," he said.

"Gladly, my friend," the princess replied. "But you have done me a great service and must be rewarded. And I cannot allow such a perfect team to be broken up."

And so Karlis and his men were named to Princess Evelina's new council and given a large plot of land near the palace. There they built a castle and settled down, though Karlis often went off to explore the world. Princess Evelina shared some of his adventures—but those are stories for another book.

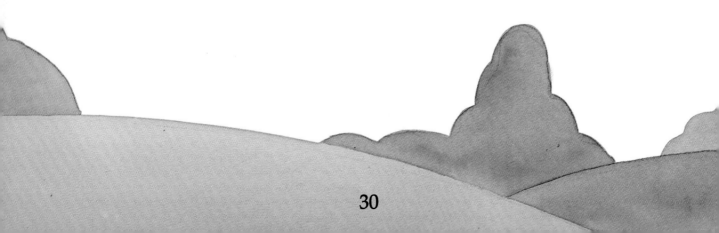

Clever Karlis is a legend from Latvia, a small country in northeastern Europe. Latvia has a rich and varied history. Archaeological evidence shows that this part of the Baltic region was first inhabited in the early Stone Age. By the middle of the Bronze Age, Latvia was an important link in the trade routes between southern and northern Europe.

Latvia was ruled by the Soviet Union from 1940 to 1991. During that time the Latvian people strived to maintain their own culture, language, and historical traditions. When the Soviet Union finally disintegrated, Latvia became an independent country once more. Latvian folk arts, once forced underground, are now an important part of daily life.

Choral singing is a very popular activity in Latvia today. Many people take part in song festivals, which are held throughout the year. The folk song, or *daina,* is one of their oldest arts. In the past century, more than a million dainas have been collected from ordinary people and catalogued by Latvian researchers.

Under Soviet rule, Latvian children were forced to learn only Russian. Now they are taught in their own national language. Latvian folktales, kept alive by parents and grandparents, once more bring delight to a whole new generation of children.